Table of Content

Earthly Delights *2*

Earthly Delights

In the throes of Anne's orgasm, the almost too hot liquid continued to dribble along her clitoris and labia. Nick, her husband, was enjoying his morning cup of coffee, which mixed well with Anne's natural flavors. He had drawn this moment out, in order to maximize her pleasure. But, after he had let the last mouthful of coffee flow out over her pussy, he graciously sucked on her clit until she came, forcefully.

"Please, don't stop!" she repeated several times before keening loudly, as she was prone to do during climax.

It was their "kinky day off," which they had looked forward to for the last two weeks. The kids had just gone back to school after their summer break. Anne and Nick had gone about their usual morning routine, so that they wouldn't arouse the suspicion of their teens, who were naturally inquisitive. They both got up at the normal time, and dressed as if they were going to work.

Typically, they split the duty of dropping the kids off at their separate schools and that was exactly what they had done that morning. However, instead of driving to work after the drop off, they both went home and met in the kitchen.

Nick made it home first and was waiting with his coffee as Anne walked in from the garage. He was tall and fairly lean. Standing against the counter, his long legs were crossed at the ankle. She approached him languidly, wearing a sly smile on her face.

"Well, we did it, Babe. A whole day to ourselves," she said. Anne stopped just in front of Nick and placed her hands on his chest. He was still fully dressed, although he had loosened his tie and unbuttoned the top of his dress shirt. She rose onto her toes and attempted to kiss him. As usual, he leaned down so that she could reach his lips. Their tongues met, and a fire sparked.

Nick broke the kiss and was succinct. "Take off your clothes, slowly."

Anne was only too happy to oblige. She had worn something simple today in anticipation of the sensual outcome. Her pumps came off first. Then, she slowly unbuttoned her dress pants and wiggled her hips as she removed them. Her arms crossed in front of her and she grabbed the bottom of her shirt. Lifting slowly and uncrossing her arms, she shed her simple black top.

Anne was left standing in her sheer black boy shorts and matching bra. Nick far preferred to see Anne naked; she was very aware of that fact as she paused. Nick raised his eyebrow expectantly and Anne smirked as she leisurely removed her undergarments.

Stepping forward Nick ran his hands along her shoulders, down along her breasts and paused at her waist. She gasped as he easily lifted her after his hands had made it down to her ass. She wrapped her legs around him and reluctantly let go when he placed her in a sitting position on the kitchen island. She noticed that her already wet pussy had left a mark on his blue shirt.

They were now face to face as he stood between her legs which were widely spread. Nick grabbed Anne's hair and tilted her head up as he aggressively leaned forward to kiss her deeply. She matched his intensity and sucked his tongue into one of the three warm holes she would offer him today.

Nick pulled back, stepped away to the refrigerator and emerged with a bottle of champagne and orange juice. He poured Anne a mimosa which was very skimpy on the juice. She took the glass as he offered it to her, and drank it carefully. Nick had put his hands on either side of her hips, dipped his head down and proceeded to maul her right nipple with his mouth. It was now her turn to grab his hair and she did so to guide his head from her right nipple to her left.

Anne's nipples were very sensitive and Nick knew exactly how much force it took to drive her to the brink of an orgasm, after all, they had been together for nearly thirty years. He sucked and nipped at her tits while she started to display a rising level of excitement by throwing back her head and sputtering impassioned sounds. Her babbling continued as Nick grasped her tightly around the waist. Worried that she was unable to finish her drink due to her mounting frenzy, he eased off. Nick was usually a gentleman, until the fun and games really started.

After she had downed her mimosa and put the glass on the counter, Nick came up for air to move the glass off of the island. He returned to her quickly and stared into her hazel eyes while he reached into a kitchen drawer directly beneath Anne's ass. Two sets of handcuffs emerged and Anne eyes widened with excitement. Nick gently laid Anne down across the island. Her knees were splayed obscenely and her shapely ass was positioned just at the edge on one side. Anne's arms were stretched above her head and secured to drawer handles that lay beneath the edge of the counter. Sitting on a stool Nick found himself favorably positioned with his face close to her freshly waxed pussy. His travel coffee mug was in hand.

"I think it's time to finish my coffee," Nick said. Anne loved coffee time, even though she never drank it herself. The heat of his morning drink was far warmer than body temperature and it always took her clitoris a few moments to acclimate while it tried to decide if it was too hot, too cool, or just right... kind of like Goldilocks.

Nick took a long swig and held it in his mouth for a few moments before swallowing. Leaning down, he sucked on Anne's clit while the heat from the coffee was still affecting his lips and tongue. Anne cried out from the intensity of the temperature and the vigor with which he pulled at the most sensitive part of her body. She also noted that he hadn't shaved today, and the feeling of his facial stubble on her pussy provided extra stimulant. Just when he sensed she was about to spiral into an orgasm, he released her clit and took another swig. Unhurriedly, Nick dribbled hot coffee down her clit and labia. His tongue lapped at the hot liquid and struck out into her sopping wet cunt.

He repeated the process several times which brought the mighty climax out of his wife. It started deep within the walls of her cunt, and spread out through her entire pelvis. At the last minute, Nick had resumed sucking on her clit while he penetrated her with two of his fingers and began to massage her G-spot. She cried out as her pussy convulsed and her legs tremored. Anne's eyes were squeezed shut as her arms struggled against the unyielding restraints. Nick knew she would have brought them down to grab at her own nipples, had they been free. But, that pleasure would have to wait.

Nick sat back and chuckled as Anne caught her breath. He was quite masterful at playing her body to achieve sexual bliss, and this was just the start of a very long day.

"Little One, it's time to take this party outside," Nick announced as he rose to unlock the cuffs from the drawer handles, but not from Anne's wrists. She sat upright, slowly, and Nick poured her another very generous mimosa. Luckily, the weather was perfect for a naked romp outside. It was sunny and already 78 degrees. Nick divested himself of his clothing quickly since he was rather jacked up after having his face in Anne's inviting pussy for the last ten minutes. His wife eyed him lustily while she finished her second drink.

"I can't wait any longer, just fuck me now, please," whined Anne. She leaned over a kitchen stool, stood on her tippy toes and parted her legs so that Nick could see her wet cunt. Reaching behind her, Anne pulled apart her cheeks and uncovered her delicate appearing anus. It literally took every bit of restraint that Nick contained to decline her shameless offer.

"Come on, Babe. I have a special surprise for you out back," Nick said, after taking several deep breaths. His cock stood at complete attention, veins bulging, with a pearly liquid visible at the tip. Anne smiled sweetly, popped up and bounded out the patio door into the great outdoors.

Their backyard was idyllic. An expansive saltwater pool was the centerpiece. Beyond the pool on the right side of the yard was a gazebo which Anne initially felt was too traditional. However, it had been put to good use a few nights prior during a "kinky evening," when the kids had been occupied at the movies.

On the other side of the yard, past the pool, stood a large freestanding stone fireplace that rose about ten feet in the air. It had rounded side walls that were about three feet tall and extended ten feet on both sides.

Their backyard was fairly private with a wooded area on all sides. If neighbors had wanted to snoop, they could. But, Anne didn't really care.

Her parents had been teenage hippies when she was born in the late 60s. While there had been many downsides to her early life, it did leave her with two distinctive qualities. The first was an unparalleled knowledge base of Grateful Dead music, which was rarely useful.

More interesting was Anne's complete acceptance of nudity as a natural state. She was very comfortable walking around the house, both inside and out, completely nude. It wasn't that she had a killer bod. Many men would have found her lacking, since she was far from curvy. Anne was a very petite woman, in all respects. But, she was well proportioned for her size. At 96 pounds, her breasts, belly and ass had minimal, but present curves. Luckily for her, Nick loved tiny women.

Her kids were well aware of her inclination and didn't give it a second thought except when they were bringing friends home for a visit. Then, a warning call was always made in advance. She was very respectful of the fact that others might not share her predilection. Just in case she was caught unprepared when the front doorbell rang, a very casual, loose-fitting dress hung in a closet in the front hall.

Anne was also very at ease with the nudity of others. That may have played into her decision to become a medical doctor. The complexity of the human body fascinated her at all levels. An added benefit was that her very casual attitude about nudity seemed to relax some of her more anxious patients.

While Anne didn't particularly care if someone saw her naked while walking around her house or backyard, she wasn't jazzed about people watching her have sex. She and Nick were very careful to only engage in outdoor activities on days when they knew their landscapers and pool men wouldn't be working. Today was no exception. They reveled in the fact that they had their own yard completely to themselves, as funny as that sounds.

As she stood on the deck, waiting for her husband to catch up, she jingled her handcuffs noisily.

"Do I still need these, Babe?" "Oh yeah, you do. Today, I have a new game," replied Nick, who was not usually this cagey. Anne couldn't help but notice that in his hand, Nick carried the key chain that held the keys to all of their bondage equipment. She wondered what laid in store for her and hoped it was something terribly rough.

While Nick had introduced Anne to bondage very early in their relationship, he never could have imagined the way she would take to it, and even more deviant practices. They had started dating as first year medical students, when funds were tight. The two had made do with ties, shoelaces, cheap rope and a homemade whiffle ball mouth gag (which they still had, for sentimental reasons).

When they were in a more comfortable financial situation, they graduated to handcuffs, metal chains, ceiling hooks, stockades and any other kinky device they thought might be worth a try.

Where the early days were strictly about bondage, Anne had discovered she was a bit of a masochist and deeply enjoyed spankings, floggings, wax play and electric stimulation. Canings were a bit of a grey zone, depending on Nick's level of exuberance.

For his part, Nick was a "reluctant sadist." Causing pain was not something he initially enjoyed. Nick was a tall, sturdy, fun loving guy. But, he was happy to go above and beyond in order to satisfy Anne's initial desires and then, her needs. As time went on, he grew more comfortable with inducing pain because it really did bring Anne great pleasure and seemed to magnify her sexual high. Eventually, he also realized that it was arousing for him to watch his wife wince and cry out from whatever method of pain he decided to inflict. Red angry marks on her ass got his cock hard, fast.

As Anne left the deck and wandered out past the pool, waiting for Nick to catch up, she could feel her anticipation soaring. They had several pool recliners on the far side of the deck with tables set between them. Nick took his time lumbering over and dropped the keys on one of the small tables. "I wouldn't want these to get lost in the grass," said Nick, while smiling. He could always be counted on to be aware of potential hazards.

Anne noticed a bag of "supplies" sitting on one of the Adirondak chairs in front of the fireplace. Nick walked over, grabbed the bag and turned to her.

"I didn't get out here before the sprinkler system started, so we're going to be behind the fireplace, where it's still dry." Nick shrugged. He was always able to adapt to circumstances, should a plan go awry. Anne figured his initial strategy involved a more central location, and made a mental note to ask him about it later.

Nick carried the supplies over to Anne, took her by her hair and led her to a dry patch of grass behind the stone fireplace. He told her to sit, and she obediently complied, even though Nick knew she was internally shuddering at the thought of ants and worms having potential contact with her crotch. She maintained her cool, sat cross-legged, and tried to look into the bag.

The first items Nick pulled out of the bag were four small caliber metal rods that appeared to be about 8 inches long and had a loop at one end.

"Watcha got there, Babe?" inquired Anne.

"Tent stakes. I don't believe we've ever restrained you directly to the ground."

"Oh! Can I lie on a towel, instead of the grass?" Anne sounded hopeful, but knew the answer in advance.

"No, you may not. It's going to be a rough ride all the way around." Nick was very firm in his response, which made Anne's pussy juice double in volume. She swooned when he was this rigid, literally and figuratively. His cock, she noted greedily, remained fully erect.

Nick took two of the tent stakes, and reached into the bag for a hammer. He positioned her as desired, running perpendicular to the back of the fireplace arms up and out to the sides. Then, Nick hammered the stakes into the ground beyond her wrists, secured the chain running between the handcuffs to each stake and closed both parts of the cuff to the same wrist. Cuffs went around her ankles and the same procedure was performed.

In the end, Anne was left on her back and all four limbs were stretched as far as possible, away from her body. She appeared somewhat uncomfortable and that was exactly the intent. Nick's eyes were immediately drawn to her tits. Even though she was not a large breasted woman, she had nipples that were absolutely perfect. When erect, they were the shape of small raspberries, and only slightly lighter in color. Nick greatly enjoyed teasing them because they were so sensitive.

Falling to his knees, Nick lowered his body over Anne's. He licked her nipples gently before enveloping them in his warm, loving mouth.

Anne relaxed somewhat during his ministrations, but knew the undiluted pleasure would not last. After several moments, Nick raised his body and reached over to his bag. She heard the clanking of chains before she saw the dreaded clover clamps. After giving a final pinch to her nipples with his fingers, he placed the clamps directly on the buds which were exquisitely sensitive at that point.

As often as Nick used the clover clamps, Anne couldn't seem to get used to the severity of their grip. She breathed deeply and slowly until her poor, abused nipples were numb from the constriction. As it was, she was glad that she was restrained so tightly, because to move while wearing the clamps was even more punishing.

Instead of thinking about what she knew was coming, Anne looked up at the blue sky, which was dotted with fluffy clouds. Thankfully the sun wasn't directly overhead, so the temperature was perfect. A tickle on her wrist caught her attention and Anne looked over in horror at a big black ant crawling up her left arm. When it came to physical and mental stress, Anne was a fierce warrior. But, when it came to insects, she would scream and run with the most girly of girls.

"Babe! Get it off! Fuck! Ahhhh! Ugh! Goddamnit!" Anne hollered with no humor in her voice. Nick's face was impassive as he flicked the offending insect off her wrist. He skimmed his tongue up Anne's arm to get her back into the mental state of an obedient fuck toy. It worked quickly, and he touched his lips to her forehead while murmuring "let's get back to business."

Anne knew what would follow and braced herself. Nick had attached an additional clamp to the clover clamps some time ago. As he scooted back on his knees, his attention turned to her engorged clit. It was completely uncovered due to the position of her legs. At first, he played nice and licked sweetly at her sensitive center. But, that was not to last, and he abruptly pinched her clit in the clamp as she called out his name, frantically.

The three clamps were attached in the middle by an "O" ring. Nick grabbed the ring and yanked upward, which further caused Anne to tense, grunt and pant heavily. Anne squirmed beneath the gleam in her beloved husband's eyes.

Nick leaned down and whispered in Anne's ear.

"Little One, you are completely at my mercy. What shall I do with you?" Nick's lips grazed her ear as he spoke, which caused her to shiver, despite the warm weather. "There's a puckered star down there that looks very empty."

Nick dipped his finger in Anne's pussy as a way of teasing her, and also for lubrication. She had plenty of juiced pooled in that space from their morning activities. When his fingers were coated in her nectar, they moved south, down to her as yet, unused warm hole.

Anne inhaled sharply as he rubbed his first two fingers around the outside, gently at first. He began to prod and poke a bit deeper after a moment or two. Anne loved anal sex and her whimpers took on a desperate tone. Nick's fingers were long, thick and soon violated her most private slot, just as she had craved. He inserted them to their base and pumped them both into her ass, in synch. But, his tact changed and he began to alternate the fingers so that as one was diving in, the other was easing out.

At the same time, Nick placed two fingers from his left hand as far into her pussy as he could manage. Rotating from side to side, his left hand massaged her hot, needy cunt. Eventually he turned so that the hand in her pussy faced down and applied a great deal of posterior pressure onto the tissue which separated her cunt from her ass. The fingers on his right hand continued to piston away in her lower tunnel.

Anne was driven mad by the pulsations in her ass and the unrelenting pressure in her pussy. She was calling out "Please don't stop!" yet again as he continued. Just when he noted she was on the brink of orgasmic rapture, he bent down and gave another yank on the nipple/clit clamps by grabbing the "O" ring with his teeth and pulling hard.

Anne spiraled out of control as she felt the complex orgasm sweep through her body. Pressure to the posterior wall of her pussy always induced uncontrolled leg shaking climaxes (Nick called them "body rocks") and today was no exception. The clamps on her nipples and clit had added enough dynamite to blow up a train... and boy did she explode. In short, it was the perfect trifecta. Her bondage magnified the climax since she literally had no room for movement. Every muscle in her body contracted at the same time just before her ass and pussy clamped down brutally on his fingers. Small muscle spasms followed and Anne thrashed as much as her restraints allowed.

Anne called out at the top of her lungs until the crest had passed. Nick knew that if neighbors were out and about, there would have been no way they would have missed her howls. At that moment, he didn't care. Her wave of pleasure swept him along for the ride.

Finally, Anne settled and looked her husband in the eye with complete devotion. She fought to catch her breath but did so, eventually.

She tilted her head back and closed her eyes as she spoke. "Thanks Babe. I think it's your turn, now. How can I make you happy, Luv?"

Nick knew, in this position, the fastest way to relieve his painfully raging erection was to go for Anne's mouth. He moved up and straddled her chest with his knees, while he grabbed her by the hair and pulled up on her head. With a savage ferocity, he thrust his dick straight down Anne's throat, causing her eyes to pop open when she immediately gagged. He pulled out enough to let her take a breath before he shoved his cock down again, and again, relentlessly. Anne had a talent for deep throating and once she had adjusted, took him to the hilt without further incident. She would have preferred to wrap her arms around his thighs, but was still bound.

It didn't take Nick long, since he had been primed from working on Anne earlier. Instead of coming in her mouth, he pulled out, shifted back slightly, and jerked off in her face and on her neck. Semen spewed out onto her hair, eyes and cheeks. Into her mouth and nostrils flew trails of the white, warm liquid. His orgasms were quiet and typically had a stealth quality. But today, he sighed loudly as he came, especially when he saw his wife's face painted white.

When the last drop of cum fell right onto the notch at the base of her throat, Nick promptly moved back and lowered his weight to rest on Anne's small frame. Since Anne still had the clamps on her lady parts, she squealed until he rolled over onto his back next to her. He rested his head in the crook of her arm and turned his body to face hers. They both lay and huffed for several minutes, until the euphoria had passed.

Nick pulled his head up, peered down at Anne's semen covered face and smiled. "I'm guessing you want to take a dip in the pool now?" he asked quietly, while using his fingers to smear the cum over her cheeks, like face paint.

Anne giggled. "I'll do whatever you want, Babe. That was amazing."

"I'm happy to have a satisfied customer." Nick looked down at her with laughing eyes. He glanced over her body and decided to remove the clamps first, since they were quite harsh. Anne screeched as each of the clamps was removed and then immediately relaxed her body. Nick realized he should pick up the pace when he noticed the sun had caused his cum to dry quickly on her face and hair.

Pulling up on the stakes, Nick was able to free her limbs with minimal exertion. Anne took a minute to appreciate the physics of the situation, since she had been unable to raise the stakes due to the angle of her extremities. She was a bit stiff, and noticed that she made quite a jingle jangle as she moved her arms and legs since they still sported the metal cuffs. However, she soon managed to sit up on the grass.

Quite suddenly, their heads jerked at the same time, when they heard a heart stopping sound.

"Come on, they aren't home. Don't sweat it," shouted a voice that was well known to them both.

Ryan was 21 and a college student. His parents were very close friends of Anne and Nick. They had literally known him for his entire life. Ryan was a few years older than their oldest son and they had carpooled with the other family for several years, back and forth to the boys' school.

Anne and Nick froze in place and rapidly took stock of the situation. Anne was naked and her face and hair were covered in drying semen. She was still shackled and the keys to the cuffs lay on a table that was out in the open. They had no towel, because of Nick, she noted dourly. Nick, similarly naked, was certainly the more presentable of the two. He also had the benefit of being entirely sober. Anne was feeling a bit tipsy from her two drinks.

"Are you sure? I'm not in the mood to get busted out here. I know we're going to get caught eventually. We've just been lucky so far," said a second male voice that was also easy to identify. Sean was Ryan's best friend and lived close by. He sounded appropriately nervous about trespassing in Anne and Nick's back yard oasis.

"Bro, I saw them both leave for work this morning. I'm telling you we're in the clear. Anne took the girls, and Nick took the boys. We have all day, if we need it. It worked out great the last couple of times. It's the perfect place to hang out," said Ryan, much to the horror of Anne and Nick.

"Whatever, if they come home, you can take the fall," replied Sean, who sounded more resigned to the situation than he had at first.

Nick leaned down and whispered in Anne's ear. "Ok, this is hilarious," It took a lot to shake Nick, who was naturally a jovial guy.

"WHAT. THE. FUCK!" Anne was shocked, but managed to keep her voice barely audible. Her cum covered face was affecting her mood greatly. "What should we do? Jesus! Shit!" Anne usually had a pretty good sense of humor when it came to kids. But, she was unhappy that the young men were using their backyard for hijinks while they weren't home.

"Now THIS will make for a great story someday," Nick replied, in a hushed tone. His eyes were alight with mirth, which Anne shunned.

Anne's eyes narrowed and she barked at Nick, as much as she could while using a low voice, "What are they doing? Go peek!" Anne would have gone herself, but was nervous about making noise with her wrist and ankle jewelry.

Nick army crawled up towards the half wall on the side of the fireplace nearest the pool. He slowly raised his body so that he could peer over and scope out the two interlopers. His eyes widened in surprise. Glancing back at Anne, he grimaced.

After dragging his body back to Anne, he debated about whether he should be truthful about the situation. "They're by the side of the pool... naked."

Anne's face dropped as her mind wrapped around this current information. Not only were she and her husband nude, but so were the young men. Going off on an alcohol fueled tangent, she found the update curious, because she hadn't picked up on a gay vibe from either boy, and wondered why they had shed their clothes.

Music started from beyond the wall; Ryan was very familiar with their outdoor sound system. Both Nick and Anne rolled their eyes and kicked themselves for not thinking to play music during their own interlude. Nick briefly considered whether he was losing his edge, but one look at Anne, in her current state, had him feeling more secure.

Ryan had picked the Reggae mix, and Shaggy's "In the Summertime" was the first up on the list. The two guys didn't play it loudly, just at the level of background noise. Nick nodded his head in approval at their choice, while Anne scowled at him. She had laid back down, flat on her back. Reluctantly, she admitted to herself and Nick that she maybe, kinda, sorta, wanted to see, for herself, what was happening.

Anne mouthed to Nick "hold onto my ankle cuffs," while she grabbed the tent stakes hanging from her wrist cuffs in her own hands. In an exaggerated way, she rolled over and tried to snake forward on her belly, to the edge of the wall. Nick chuckled as he watched her ass shimmy. Slowly, Anne raised her head up to do some recon. The two young men were about forty feet away and mostly facing the pool. They were both nude, and despite Anne's best intention, she couldn't help but notice their very fit bodies. Both Ryan and Sean were muscular, having been lacrosse players in high school and college. The muscles weren't a surprise to Anne, but seeing them nude put her in a quandary. She was as old as their mothers and close friends with both women. Surely, she should not be interested in their naked bodies. However, she was able to make out the profile of their more private areas, and nodded in appreciation.

"What time is Kayla coming?" said Sean.

Ryan replied, "She should already be here. But I have to drop her off at work in 45 minutes, so we don't have a lot of time."

Kayla was Ryan's current girlfriend and Anne hated her. She was only moderately attractive and dumb as a stone. To make matters even worse, her manners were horrible. She felt Ryan could do much better and told Ryan so on a few occasions. Ryan would only smile and reply that Kayla was "special," which made Anne want to vomit.

Nick had crawled back over to the wall and was stationed near Anne, behind a large pot of flowers at the end of the wall extension. He was not surprised when Anne looked at him and mouthed "Double fuck." He shared Anne's opinion of Kayla.

They both lowered their heads and looked at each other as if searching for an obvious answer that was just out of reach. However, both Anne and Nick came up empty. If they had tried to make a run for the woods, it was unlikely they would go unnoticed at this point because of the cuffs on Anne. Nick could strike out on a solo mission, but that would leave Anne on her own if discovered, and he was too much of a gentleman to do that.

"Stay put," mouthed Anne, as if reading Nick's mind. She had hoped both "boys" would jump in the pool, which might give them an opportunity to make it to the woods together. Anne wasn't quite sure how she would manage running while her ankles dragged tent stakes, but it seemed like the best option.

The guys had spread out towels onto the poolside chairs. Sean pulled car keys out of the pocket of his swim trunks which he had deposited on the chair as well. He bent over to put them on the side table and paused. "Are these yours?" he asked of Ryan.

Anne and Nick looked on in shock as Sean picked up the set of cuff keys that was lying on the side table.

Sean added, "They look like handcuff keys. Are they for later?"

Ryan laughed, "No, those aren't mine. I think they're probably Anne and Nick's."

"Riiiight, are they playing cops and robbers, or something?" Sean rolled his eyes as he spoke.

"Not quite. I'm pretty sure they're into some kinky shit." replied Ryan, nonchalantly.

"No fucking way. How do you know?" asked Sean, incredulously.

"Well, I might have seen them using cuffs a couple of nights ago," said Ryan vaguely.

Sean's mouth dropped open. "Holy crap! You're kidding, right? They're, like, old."

"So, a few nights ago, I came over for a swim and saw them in the gazebo. They were getting it on, big time." Ryan admitted reluctantly.

Anne thought back to their outdoor sex romp from two nights ago and couldn't help smiling to herself. It was dusk as she and Nick had gone out to play in the gazebo that night. Anne had been asking Nick to turn the very cliche gazebo into an outdoor bar for several years. Nick never had the motivation to make the change, but had long planned to put it to good use. That night, his plans came to fruition.

During dinner on the night in question, Anne had pointed out that the kids would be gone for hours. She let the implication hang. Nick, being quick on the draw, asked Anne if she was in the mood to play, to which she replied, "Why yes, I am."

After dinner that night, Nick had instructed Anne to meet him, naked, in the gazebo. He went upstairs to gather some things while she undressed and went outside. The gazebo was white, and octagonal. It was open on all sides and had a shingled roof. There was a waist length railing that had regularly spaced spindles running from the railing to the floor. About 8 inches down from the ceiling was another decorative railing, which also had spindles that ran from the roof to the upper railing.

Anne waited for Nick patiently in the gazebo and was surprised to see him approach while still fully dressed. He pulled cuffs out of his pockets and tethered her wrists to the upper railing and her ankles to the lower railing. Her upper and lower extremities were spaced as far apart as possible, and Anne had to stand on her toes to accommodate the stretch from her arms being attached so far above her head. A bit gag came out of his other pocket and was placed in Anne's mouth. She looked back in time to see him taking his belt off and immediately she felt weak in the knees, not from fear, but excitement... of a sexual nature.

Nick had his belt looped in one hand, as he stood behind Anne, who was facing out of the gazebo. With his other hand he reached around and grabbed her left nipple and pinched, hard. Her vocalization was highly muted due to the bit gag in her mouth.

"Have you been a good girl?" Nick asked, while his lips brushed her right ear?

Anne shook her head, indicating that she had not, even though that was clearly not the case. Nick informed her that the gazebo would come in handy as he pulled away from her naked trembling body. "You get ten lashes tonight, Little One."

After he took several steps back, Nick wielded the leather belt against Anne's very white ass. Generally, Anne did not like to be spanked while hanging from her hands, and suspended on her toes. If the hits weren't perfectly centered, her body wrenched unpredictably. Because of the waist height railing, she was more stable in the gazebo and Nick didn't have to worry about unintended torque.

The first strike was in the middle of the intensity spectrum and Anne had almost choked since he usually started out gently. Nick was a pro at making use of her entire ass for their spanking sessions. Each hit was well spaced, but that night, he was more forceful than normal and as a result, Anne grunted, groaned and would have cried out, but for her bit gag. As always, the last strike was different. He used an underhand motion to flick the belt against her vulva and clit. The pain was delicious. Tears were falling from her eyes when he was done, and she was desperate for an orgasm.

Thick fingers plunged into her pussy as she remained tied to the building. "What's this? Do you want me to fuck you now?"

"Essss," was all she could manage with the gag in her mouth.

Anne heard Nick's zipper and felt his heat as he moved in more closely. Abruptly, he filled her cunt, but only for a few seconds, while he coated his dick her overflowing juices. After pulling out, he lined his cock up with her ass, and moved forward, while placing his right hand securely over her lower abdomen.

All of Anne's weight shifted to her handcuffed wrists to try and slow his invasion. She really did love anal sex and this was one of her favorite positions because it seemed so raw. Anne squealed loudly as he breeched her outer sphincter and halted at her inner sphincter. Because Nick knew Anne's body so well, he paused until she had relaxed enough for him to continue. Forward he went, to the hilt. Anne made some type of garbled noise just before she had begun to moan as his thighs came in contact with the burning skin on her ass.

Soon she was producing unmistakable sounds of pleasure. Anne swayed to and fro as much as possible as Nick plowed into her ass. He moved one hand to her right tit and squeezed roughly while his other hand moved to her clit and began to slowly move in circles. Every few seconds, he would lower his fingers and penetrate her pussy.

It really didn't take long for her body to rock from a powerful orgasm. He licked and kissed and sucked on her neck while her body writhed in front of his. Nick felt all of her muscles tighten just before they detonated in waves of pulsing energy that caused him to lose control and come wildly while spurting semen into her ass.

Anne's fond reminiscence slowly morphed into a feeling of shock as she realized that Ryan had been watching them. He had very likely seen Nick restrain Anne, beat her ass with a belt and then sodomize her. And, Ryan had also likely noted that Anne loved every minute of it. Briefly, she wondered what the young man had made of their escapade and whether he would tell his friend exactly what he had seen. Anne had just met his mother for drinks the night before, and it wasn't awkward, so she felt confident he had not spilled the beans at home.

As predicted, Sean asked, "What were they doing with the handcuffs? I bet Anne tied up Nick, right? I could see her taking the lead because Nick is so mellow. Did you take video?"

Ryan managed to say "No! I didn't take video, but..." just as Kayla bounded around the corner at a full run.

"Sorry, I'm late! God, I love it here; it's the perfect place for a hook-up." She ran around the pool and right up to Ryan, who had moved closer to the water. She kissed him passionately, while he slipped the straps from her yellow sundress down over her shoulders. Her arms wrapped around his head as the dress lowered past her hips.

Anne and Nick stared on in disbelief as Sean approached Kayla from behind and squatted down. He finished lowering the dress to her ankles and proceeded to rub his hands up and down her legs. After he transitioned to his knees, he put his face right at the base of Kayla's buttocks and started to lick her skin.

Kayla groaned and she twisted to look down and back at Sean. "Hey Baby, I've missed you too. Come up here and give me a kiss." Sean rose and Kayla was suddenly naked and sandwiched between two very muscular and well hung men. She turned her head to the side as Sean met her mouth with searing hot kisses as he grabbed her blond ponytail. Ryan had started fondling her breasts and Kayla's moans soon became audible.

Ironically, the tables had turned; Anne and Nick now felt like illicit voyeurs in their own backyard. It was very clear that the threesome was about to engage in, well, a threesome. Anne realized this must have been what Ryan meant when he said Kayla was "special" and smirked. However, Anne noted that she was not one to take the moral high ground, since she had often fantasized about group sex over the years. Anne tried to close her eyes and avoid the porn show that was taking place in front of her, but the dried semen on her face had become a bit stiff. It was far more comfortable to leave her eyes open. She could have moved back, behind the wall, but turnabout was fair play. It seemed that Ryan had seen Nick pleasure Anne sexually and in a very deviant way. This seemed like a case of karma.

The older couple watched the young adults. The three were a swirling vortex of hands and their panting had become quite heavy. Kayla broke the momentum and spoke up. "Let's move to a lounge chair. I want you both at the same time, like last week." She grabbed Ryan and Sean by their protruding cocks and led them over to the chair that was farthest away from the hidden pair.

Kayla knelt on the chair, which was laid flat. Bending over, her pussy was exposed and available. It was clear to the married couple that Kayla was bald and dripping wet even though they were fifty feet away. Ryan moved forward and Anne watched as he inserted several fingers into her pussy. Kayla made a mewing sound that conveyed indescribable pleasure as he slowly massaged her moist cunt.

In the back of her mind, Anne compared Ryan's technique to that of her husband. There was no contest. Even from a distance, Anne could see that the younger man lacked the finesse that her husband had acquired over his lifetime. Where Ryan used one hand, Nick would have used two, to heighten the pleasure by a several fold factor. Nick would have licked Anne's back, and even nibbled at the skin on her shoulder, had she been on that chair. He might have grabbed at her hair and used his body weight to hold her position. What was certainly true was that while Kayla and Ryan seemed to be enjoying themselves, they still had a lot to learn.

Sean moved around to Kayla's head and also got on his knees in front of her, on the recliner. He held his dick in his hand and grabbed Kayla by the side of her head, with his free hand. His dick entered her mouth and he proceeded to pummel her face, while Ryan continued to finger her from behind.

Once she appeared to be accustomed to the large cock in her mouth, Ryan straddled the chair from behind and plunged his dick into her pussy. The men rocked back and forth, alternating. It reminded Anne of a seesaw, a very bawdy seesaw.

Kayla crooned as much as possible, with her throat was full of cock. Both men appeared to be intent on their rhythm. Anne felt herself getting more and more wet between her own legs and she could see that her husband was fully erect, again. She knew she must have been a terrible site with dried cum all over her face and grass in her hair. But, when Nick looked down at her, she could see his unadulterated lust. Anne looked Nick head on and gave her best come hither look.

Their imminent plans were interrupted by Kayla's rather loud orgasm. Anne and Nick popped the tops of their heads just over the stone wall again. Kayla's body was jerking madly. Ryan and Sean were groaning and Ryan gave in first. He halted his rocking and shouted out "Fuck!" It was clear that he was unloading cum into her pussy. Sean seemed to be taking it all in with wide eyes. Kayla had released Sean's dick from her mouth as she climaxed (Anne rolled her eyes at the amateur move), so he was left hanging. After Kayla gathered her wits, she told him to "come inside me from behind," and he moved back to her cunt. It took but a few strokes and he paused while his body shook from the tremors of his own orgasm.

The three on the chair collapsed on each other. Kayla was on her side with her knees drawn up to her chest. Anne could see the cum mixture drizzling out of her pussy. Ryan had his knees on the ground and his head on her shoulder. Sean was similarly situated, but from behind and had his head on her hip. The trio took several minutes to compose themselves, while Anne and Nick sank back down to the grass.

A cell phone started to ring on the side of the pool. Kayla announced, "It's me, I'll get it."

Anne peeked back up and saw her saunter over to her phone, which was in the pocket of her sundress.

"Yes, I'm on my way now." said Kayla. She hung up and said, "Guys, I have to get going."

Ryan groaned, "Shit, we just got started."

"Do we have time for a quick dip in the pool?" said Sean.

Kayla replied, "I can't get my hair wet, but I can wade into the shallow end."

Ryan and Sean stood and both took running jumps into the deep end of the pool. They surfaced while laughing and swam to the opposite end. Kayla had eased herself down the steps and Anne frowned as she imagined the cum seeping from Kayla's pussy into the pool.

Perhaps, she thought to herself, she could have the pool cleaners make an extra trip out this week. On the other hand, the pool was big enough that the semen would easily be diluted.

After spending several minutes frolicking in an asexual way, the three emerged from the water. They dried off with their own towels and re-dressed. Grabbing hands, the three walked up the hill and around the side of the house. As the young lovers exited, the old lovers were left still hidden in their own yard.

Anne and Nick faced each other. "Wow, our back yard has seen a lot of action lately." said Anne.

"Maybe we should start charging by the hour. We could post a sign with the rates." Nick joked.

Anne looked at Nick and he returned the stare, trying to gauge her mood. When he leaned over and kissed her semen covered face, he knew he had guessed right as she grabbed his head and pulled him down. She straddled him through a chorus of clanking tent stakes and leaned over to whisper in his ear... "Let's head up to the bedroom," she said, provocatively.

"Shower first," said Nick, with no room for argument. Anne felt her pelvis contract with his directive, and she knew there was more fun in her immediate future.

They stood, shaking their heads in amusement and started to walk towards the house "Ryan really should have turned off the sound system. Maybe I'll call him and tell him to come back," Nick said while "Boombastic" played in the background.

As if on cue, Ryan came tearing around the side of the house at a full run. He froze in place as he saw Anne and Nick walking away from the fireplace and around the pool. It was as if time paused as the three people stared at each other. Ryan's mouth dropped open as he realized that Anne and Nick must have seen the sexual interlude that he had just shared with Kayla and Sean.

Nick stepped in front of Anne to shield her from Ryan's widely open eyes, but Anne stepped back around him. No one said a word. They just looked back and forth at each other, and reviewed their options.

Finally, Anne gulped, "Ryan, what if we all pretend this never happened. Nick and I will never speak of this to anyone as long as you can promise the same about what you may have seen here the other night.

"Deal," replied Ryan after taking a deep breath, staring at the handcuffs.

"I think you should leave now," said Anne.

Ryan didn't even hesitate before he turned around and high-tailed it out of the yard. He and his parents were supposed to come for dinner this weekend. Anne anticipated an awkward evening. For now, she just wanted to head inside and take a shower. The day was still young, and there was plenty of time for more kinky fun.

Printed in the USA
CPSIA information can be obtained
at www.ICGtesting.com
LVHW042155041124
795721LV00027B/493